D1528306

The Secret Heroes

Carla Mishek and Margo Sorenson

Perfection Learning®

Inside Illustration: Dan Hatala
Design: Tobi Cunningham
Cover Image: Corbis

Dedications

For my grandmothers who encouraged me to write when I was a child. For Ron, my forever muse, whose help was beyond measure. For Mom, my other relatives, and pals who bolstered my efforts and hopes. You know who you are. My gratitude is endless. For my memorable students through the years. For the friendship and bond of my coauthor, I extend deep thanks. If only our Sam and Sachi could reach around the world and crown it with the respect and understanding they discovered in each other.   —C. M.

For my dear family—Jim, Jane and Chris, Matt and Jill—who are my heroes too! For Carla, dear coauthor, who persevered through all.   —M. S.

Printed in the United States of America.
For information, contact
Perfection Learning® Corporation,
1000 North Second Avenue,
P.O. Box 500,
Logan, Iowa 51546-0500.
Phone: 1-800-831-4190 • Fax: 1-800-543-2745
RLB ISBN-13: 978-0-7569-1260-4
RLB ISBN-10: 0-7569-1260-1
PB ISBN-13: 978-0-7891-5992-2
PB ISBN-10: 0-7891-5992-9
2 3 4 5 6 7 PP 18 17 16 15 14 13
perfectionlearning.com
Printed in the U.S.A.

Table *of* Contents

1
No Zaydeh for Sam

Sam watched the kids in his new
fifth-grade class. They were yelling
and cheering during their recess game.
"Go, Jack, go!"

"Home run, Jack!"

Thwack! The ball sailed through the air. It was a home run!

"Way to go, Jack!"

That would never happen to Sam. He would never hit a home run. He wasn't a baseball player.

Sam could draw. But that wasn't important, no matter what his grandpa, **Zaydeh**, always used to say.

Sam shoved his hands into his jeans pockets. He leaned back against the tree at the edge of the baseball diamond and sighed.

It was bad enough being a new kid at school. He just couldn't go out there and look stupid too. That would sure put the **kibosh** on making new friends.

Sam thought a minute. What had Zaydeh always told Sam to do when he had a problem? "Don't be afraid to ask for help, Sam," he always said.

But there was no Zaydeh now. And

Sam didn't know anyone to ask for help.

Sam took a deep breath and sank to the grass. He picked up his pencil and sketchbook and began to draw. The kids' voices floated through the air.

"Good steal, Jack!"

"Who's up next?"

Sam drew them hitting the ball, running, and swinging the bat. He drew the pitcher as she wound up.

Thwack! The bat connected with the ball again.

"You've got it! You've got it, Sachi!"

She caught the fly ball and grinned.

"Good catch, Sachi!"

All the kids could catch and throw. They could hit too. They would probably laugh at him if he tried to play baseball. Sam made a face.

Then Jack strutted up to home plate again. He swung the bat back and forth. He spit in the dirt and grinned.

Jack must think he is a really good player, Sam thought. Jack would definitely laugh at him if he tried to play baseball. Sam tapped his pencil on his sketchbook.

"But Sam, being a good artist is important too," Zaydeh had always told him. But no one cared if Sam could draw. Right now, he'd rather be playing baseball.

Sam swallowed hard. Zaydeh had been helping him hit and throw. Zaydeh helped him with so many things.

Why did Zaydeh have to die, anyway? Sam wondered as he quickly brushed his arm across his eyes.

"Don't worry, Sam," Zaydeh used to tell him when they walked to the park with their gloves and a ball. "You can learn to play baseball. You are smart enough to draw well. You're smart enough to learn to play baseball."

Practicing baseball wasn't the only

thing Sam missed about Zaydeh. There was no Zaydeh to pack good salami sandwiches with crunchy **kosher** pickles in Sam's lunch anymore. Zaydeh had even tucked a funny little note into Sam's lunch sack every day. "Don't let the **schmoes** get you down," was Sam's favorite one.

But now, there was no Zaydeh to give Sam advice about school and friends or to encourage him in his drawing.

"You'll be a real artist someday, Sam," Zaydeh had said. His eyes twinkled as he had held up Sam's latest drawing. "Keep it up. Your stuff will hang in the **Louvre**!"

There was no Zaydeh to tell Sam jokes or old stories. He especially missed those stories. Zaydeh had told stories about coming to America. He had told stories about Sam's grandma, **Bubbie**, and about Sam's mother when she was a little girl.

But the stories Sam wanted to hear over and over again were about World War II in Germany. Tears had often welled in Zaydeh's eyes when he told his stories. Sam had gripped Zaydeh's hand while they sat on the couch.

"We were put in horrible camps," Zaydeh said. "Just because we were Jews. Many, many of us died. Too many," he whispered. "But those who were lucky enough to live were brave. Even though they were prisoners, they did many brave things."

"Like what, Zaydeh?" Sam asked, even though he'd heard the stories before.

"We had to keep our spirits up," Zaydeh said. "We hid food and saved it for those who were really sick. We who were stronger took beatings and blame for the weaker prisoners. The guards could not break our spirits."

Sam squeezed his eyes shut. He could almost see the **scrawny** prisoners—dressed in ragged clothing—being beaten by the guards.

Then just as the war ended, Zaydeh and the rest of the prisoners had been set free. Sam had loved the story of how the U.S. soldiers had given the prisoners their freedom. Even though Sam knew how the story ended, it still gave him shivers.

"Tell me again, Zaydeh, how it was," Sam begged.

"Our evil Nazi guards knew the U.S. soldiers were coming to free us," Zaydeh began. "So they made us march out of the camps. They were going to hide us in the mountains. We were weak from starvation, torture, and terrible work. We were sick too. Many died in the snow. The rest of us struggled to march. We could hear huge guns thundering far away. The air was thick with smoke."

Sam could almost see the scene. He had tried to draw it lots of times. It sounded scary.

"What happened then, Zaydeh?" Sam asked, almost holding his breath.

Zaydeh continued. "I tripped and fell. I was too weak to walk anymore. I lay there thinking I would be shot. The tanks rolled closer, shaking the ground. Gunshots rang out in the darkness above me. Then I heard footsteps approaching. My heart almost stopped in fear. I knew the wicked guards would shoot anyone who couldn't walk. I knew I was about to be shot."

At this part, Sam had always squeezed Zaydeh's hand tightly, no matter how many times he had heard the story.

"And then—?" Sam asked, his mouth dry.

"Someone wiped the snow from my face. I thought it was over for me. But it was a U.S. soldier! The U.S. Army had caught up with us.

" 'Don't be afraid,' the soldier told me. 'You're free now.' " Zaydeh's eyes looked faraway. "I'll never forget him. I was too weak to walk. So he helped carry me to freedom."

Someone had taken a picture of Zaydeh and the soldier together. Sam looked at the faded picture while Zaydeh told the story.

Sam stared at the young Japanese American soldier in the American uniform with his arm around a scrawny young man. The soldier was almost holding Zaydeh up. Zaydeh was squinting as if the light was too bright.

"Tell me about him, again, Zaydeh," Sam asked.

"You can see the soldier who saved me was Japanese American." Zaydeh said, frowning. "The Japanese Americans were treated horribly by the Americans—their own countrymen."

"What happened to them?" Sam asked.

15

"They were put into prison camps," Zaydeh continued. "Just because they were Japanese. Just as we were put into prison camps because we were Jews."

"That's not right!" Sam exclaimed.

"No," Zaydeh agreed. "And the Japanese Americans fought bravely in the war—for the same country that **betrayed** them."

"I can't believe it!" Sam gulped.

"Well, the soldier invited me to move to his hometown—in America," Zaydeh said. His eyes watered behind his glasses.

16

"Several years later, I came to America. When I got off the train in the soldier's hometown, we hugged. He gave me an American flag. We planned to have a big **reunion** many years later. Our grandchildren would even come." Zaydeh smiled.

Zaydeh's smile faded. "But then Bubbie died." Zaydeh paused. "I came to live with your mother and you.

"The soldier's family wrote to me. They said he had died." Zaydeh sighed. "But I'll never forget him."

Now, Sam's zaydeh had died. There would be no more stories. Sam bit his lip.

After Zaydeh died, Sam and Mom moved back to the town where she'd grown up. It was Zaydeh's and the soldier's old hometown.

But this wasn't Sam's hometown. Here, he was in a new school where he didn't know anyone.

Sam stared again at the kids on the baseball diamond. He wanted to be out there, playing with them.

How was he going to play baseball and make friends—without Zaydeh to help him?

2
No Partner for Sam

The next morning, Sam stared at the open door of his classroom. It still didn't seem right that he couldn't talk to Zaydeh before he left for school.

"Time to **schlepp** yourself to school," Zaydeh had always joked. That was before Zaydeh's heart attack. Sam looked down at his shoes and blinked back quick tears.

Sometimes, Zaydeh used to visit Sam's old class to share some of his stories about the war. Now that Zaydeh had died, he wouldn't be telling his stories to Sam's class—or to Sam—ever again.

Other kids pushed by Sam. They talked and laughed as they hurried through the halls. Sam tightened his grip on the straps of his backpack. He thought about what had happened earlier that morning.

"Good-bye, Sam," Mom had said. She leaned over and kissed his cheek. Her perfume smelled like roses.

"Have a nice day, dear," she said. "Remember, Zaydeh's still with us—in lots of ways."

"I know. But I wish it could be like before," Sam said. He swallowed hard and opened the car door. He waved as his mom drove away.

Now Sam walked slowly to his **cubby** inside the classroom. All around him, kids were unpacking their backpacks and joking with one another. Sam kept his head down and unzipped his backpack.

Next to him, Sachi knelt down and slid books into her cubby. She looked over and smiled at Sam. Sam smiled back shyly. Something about her made him feel comfortable. She might be a good friend to have. She could sure play baseball.

But no one else noticed Sam. He took out his social studies book and his sketchbook and put away his backpack.

At his desk, he slipped his sketchbook under his book. Sachi sat in the next desk. Sam opened the book to a page and pretended to read. Maybe someone would say something to him. Maybe he would make a new friend today. Maybe even Sachi would be his friend.

"What's that?" Sachi whispered. Sam looked up. She was looking at Sam's desk. She pointed to his sketchbook. "What are you hiding under there?" Her dark brown eyes smiled at him.

Sam shoved the sketchbook farther under his book. He felt his face get warm. If she looked at the sketchbook, she would see the picture he had drawn of her! He would feel like a jerk.

"Nothing," he said. He held his breath. He couldn't look at Sachi. Would she ask to see it?

Sachi looked puzzled. "It looks like a drawing pad," she said. Then she smiled at Sam. "You can draw, can't you? I saw you drawing yesterday under the tree. Can I see? Please?" she asked.

Sam's heart thudded under his shirt. He could hear Zaydeh's voice. "Be proud of your talent. It's your **shtick**. Don't be embarrassed. An artist is special."

He looked back at Sachi. Well, maybe she wouldn't say anything mean to him about his drawings.

"Okay," he said to her. He slipped the sketchbook out from under his book. He skipped quickly past the picture he'd drawn of Sachi. He turned to a picture of Jack catching a fly ball yesterday.

Sachi's eyes opened wide. "You're good!" she exclaimed. She studied the picture. "I wish I could draw like that!"

"Thanks," Sam said. He closed the sketchbook cover. I wish I could play baseball like you, he wanted to say.

"Can I see more?" Sachi asked, reaching for the sketchbook. Sam quickly slid it under his desk. "Hey!" she said. Then she grinned.

"Let's begin, class," the teacher, Mr. Owens, said.

Whew! Sam thought. He didn't want Sachi to see he'd tried to draw her too. It was his favorite sketch from yesterday.

"I'm giving you a new project today," Mr. Owens said. He began writing on the board.

Sam watched Mr. Owens' pen squiggle purple letters across the white board. Maybe the project would be something he could draw, he hoped. He could get a good grade if he could write and draw something.

Family History Project, Sam read on the board. Oh, no! Family history—and no Zaydeh to help me, Sam thought. And Mom was so busy working. Sam held his book tighter.

"You'll interview people in your family," Mr. Owens was saying. "You can read letters and family stories that people have written. Maybe you can find out new things. You need to choose something special you can be proud of about your family. You can draw pictures and include photographs. A cover drawing will be important too," he said. "You can get help from others in the class for ideas, but the final project should be all your own work."

Good, Sam thought. He could definitely draw pictures and a great cover.

Sachi raised her hand. "What do you mean, choose something special you can be proud of?" she asked.

"Maybe your family has a tradition," Mr. Owens said. "Maybe someone in your family did something special. Maybe something important happened."

Sam saw Sachi lean over and whisper to Jack next to her, "I already know what I'm doing." Her dark eyes shone.

Jack grinned. "Yeah, me too," he said. "I think I know what I'll do my report about. My grandfather played pro baseball," he bragged. He looked around him as he said it.

Sam slid down in his desk. Great. Jack's grandfather played professional baseball. That was pretty special, all right.

What could Sam be proud of in his own family? Zaydeh had played baseball okay. He helped Sam with it. But he sure wasn't a professional. Zaydeh had worked hard all his life—but not at anything important enough for a report like this.

"And at the end," Mr. Owens was saying. Sam blinked. He had missed some of what his teacher had been saying. Uh-oh.

"When the projects are finished, we'll have Heritage Day," Mr. Owens continued. "You can wear costumes showing your family heritage." Mr. Owens smiled at the class. "If any of you have a problem figuring out a costume, just ask me for help. Then we'll invite other classes in so the other students can learn about our heritages. I'll have a special way for you to choose your partners for the day.

"We'll have a Heritage Picnic too," the teacher said. "I'll be sending a letter home to your parents about bringing some food to school that day."

Partners? Sam wondered, with a sinking feeling. He counted quickly around the class. There were 31 students. That meant one person wouldn't have a partner. He already knew who it would be.

Him.

3
Help Needed

At least the costume part of the Family Heritage Project didn't sound too hard, Sam told himself during math. He could wear his special **yarmulke**. Bubbie had embroidered one for him to wear for temple. He drew a little yarmulke at the bottom of his math paper and decorated it.

But what about the food? If only Zaydeh were here to help him with some good food. Mom was too busy to make all the good Jewish things to eat.

Zaydeh used to dabble in the kitchen after Bubbie died. Zaydeh made the best **matzo balls** ever. Sam doodled some little matzo balls next to a math problem with his pencil. And Zaydeh's chicken soup was even better than Bubbie's. Mom even thought so.

Sam drew a little soup pot around the matzo balls on his math paper. There would be no Zaydeh's chicken soup for Heritage Day, Sam sighed. Maybe he could bring jars of kosher pickles for his food instead. Mom could just buy them at the store. He drew some pickles next to the soup pot and finished his math problems just as the bell rang.

"Recess!" Mr. Owens announced.

The students began lining up in front of the door. They were pushing and shoving one another and laughing, ready to run out into the bright morning sunshine. Sam looked over at the boys in line. They elbowed one another and grinned.

"Yeah, I'll get you today!" Jack bragged. He flexed his arm and made a muscle. "Easy out," he said.

"Yeah, right," another boy answered, giving Jack a playful shove.

Sam frowned. He would never ask if he could join them. Maybe he just wouldn't play baseball—ever.

Zaydeh wouldn't have liked that, though. "Don't be too proud or too shy to ask—just try it," Zaydeh would say.

But how could he? Slowly, Sam slid his sketchbook out from under his desk and got his pencil.

"Hey!" Sam heard a voice behind him. He turned. Sachi stood behind him, holding her glove and smiling.

"Want to play baseball?" she asked. She thumped her fist in her glove.

Oh, no! Sam thought. What excuse could he make up?

"Uh, not—not today. Uh—I'd better get started on the Family Heritage Project," he fibbed. "But thanks," Sam added hastily, with a quick smile.

"Sachi! Hurry up!" a voice called.

Sachi smiled back and then headed to the line in front of the door.

Sam looked up at the writing on the board. Sure, he thought. Work on the Family Heritage Project at recess. Right. I'm definitely **meshuga**, he joked to himself. He didn't even know what he would do for the project.

Sam held his sketchbook tightly in his hands. What could he write about?

He didn't want to write just anything. He had to write about something really good.

Sam looked at everyone eagerly waiting at the door. He almost wished he had said yes to Sachi. But he wasn't good enough to play. He knew it.

Mr. Owens found his whistle and finally opened the door. The students poured out of the room. Many of them raced to the baseball diamond.

Slowly, Sam walked to the tree where he'd sat yesterday. He dropped to the grass. Maybe he could draw someone getting a hit today—maybe even Sachi again.

"Hey!" a voice said. Sam looked up. Sachi stood there, smiling. "So when are you going to play?" she asked. "You do like baseball, right? I mean, you watched us yesterday. And you're back watching today."

"Uh, yeah. But, uh, not right now," Sam hedged. "I—I'm not really watching. I'm—uh—busy." He felt a knot tie in his stomach. "Like I said, I need to work on the Family Heritage Project," he fibbed again.

"What are you going to do for the project?" she asked him.

He blinked. What was he going to do? He'd better make something up fast. "Uh—uh—I think something about my grandfather," he said quickly.

Sachi looked at him. "You are?" she said. "Me, too." She smiled. "How about playing baseball at lunch recess?" she asked.

"Maybe," Sam said slowly. He looked down at the blank page in his sketchbook.

Sachi turned to go. Then she turned back. "Did you bring a glove to school?" she asked.

Sam felt his face get hot. "Uh—no, I

didn't. I forgot." He wasn't going to bring his glove to school and make a fool of himself. Zaydeh had helped him oil it and break it in. The glove was ready, but he wasn't.

"I have an extra one," Sachi said, smiling.

"Hurry up, Sachi!" someone yelled from the diamond. "It's time to choose teams!"

"Maybe at lunch recess, then," Sachi said. She smiled at Sam. "Bye," she said. Then she turned and ran to the diamond. "I'm coming! I'm coming!" she yelled to the others.

Sam's head pounded, and his heart raced. He'd almost had to tell Sachi he wasn't any good at baseball. What an awful way to start out in a new school. Everyone would laugh at him. They'd think he was a real **schnook**. Sachi probably wouldn't laugh. But the others would.

Sam sketched as he watched and listened.

"We're gonna **scuff** you," one girl said teasingly.

Sam shut the cover of the sketchbook with a little slap. He slumped back against the scratchy tree trunk.

What about the Family Heritage Project? He'd told Sachi he was going to do it on Zaydeh. But Zaydeh wasn't nearly as exciting as having a grandfather who played pro baseball. The other kids probably wouldn't understand what made Zaydeh so special.

Sam couldn't pretend to forget to bring his baseball glove every single day. Besides, Sachi practically told him she had a glove he could borrow. What could he say to Sachi when she asked him to play baseball again? Should he ask Sachi for help? A girl? How could he ask a girl for help?

4
Proud of a Prisoner?

At lunch recess, Sam didn't go back to the tree next to the baseball diamond. What would he say to Sachi when she asked him to play again?

Instead, he walked to the far corner of the playground by the swings. He drew students pushing one another on the swings and climbing on the bars.

"Where were you at recess?" Sachi asked when they got back to class. "I thought you were going to play baseball."

Sam felt his stomach knot again. "I—uh—I went to draw people climbing on the bars," he said. He looked down at his sketchbook.

"Oh," Sachi said. She shrugged her shoulders.

"All right, class," Mr. Owens said. "It's time to start planning your projects. Take out a sheet of paper."

Everyone got to work. Sam made his list of what he needed to do for the project. During recess, he'd decided he would write about Zaydeh and his prison camp after all.

Sam would write about how brave Zaydeh and the other prisoners had been. He'd share some of the stories Zaydeh had told him about saving food and taking care of the sicker prisoners and of the wonderful **liberation**. He would tell how the U.S. Army had rescued the starving prisoners during their death march. After all, Sam was proud of his Zaydeh and how courageous he had been in the prison camp.

Sam looked up from his work. All around the classroom, kids were working together. They compared lists, talked, and laughed. Only Sam was by himself.

The week flew by. At recesses, Sam stayed away from the baseball diamond. Sachi didn't say anything more to him about playing.

Instead, Sam drew kids kicking the ball on the soccer field. He sketched them playing foursquare on the asphalt courts. He even drew some little girls sitting under a tree, playing a clapping game.

But Sam didn't draw anyone playing baseball. He didn't go anywhere near the diamond. He didn't want Sachi to ask him to play again. And he wasn't going to have everyone laugh at him when he confessed he didn't play baseball.

I'm not that dumb, Sam told himself.

Sam worked hard on his project every day after school. His mom gave him the crinkly, yellowed letters that Zaydeh's soldier friend had written. Sam read them again. He copied parts of them into his report.

Sam found the old picture of the soldier and Zaydeh. He held it tenderly. The black-and-white photo had faded to shades of brown. Sam blinked back tears as he stared at Zaydeh's face and the face of the soldier.

Something in the soldier's expression tugged at Sam's mind. What was it? Something Zaydeh had said about the soldier? He shrugged. After all, it had been a long time since he had looked at the picture. He would ask Mom if he could use it for his report.

At school, Sam worked on a picture of Zaydeh in the prison camp. Sam felt as if he had seen the camp himself. Zaydeh had told him so many times what the prison camp looked like.

The prison camp was bleak. Square, ugly buildings squatted on the dirt. Barbed wire ringed the top of the camp's brick walls. Scrawny prisoners huddled together for warmth. Guards holding rifles leered from guard towers at each corner of the camp.

Sam noticed Sachi looking over at his drawing. "That's so good," she said admiringly.

"Thanks," Sam mumbled.

"Class, I hope you're thinking about your partners for Heritage Day," Mr. Owens said. "Choose a partner whose family heritage would make an interesting match with your own. For example, you could choose a partner who has a heritage from a neighboring country. Here's another idea. Remember that people from different heritages often fought one another. You might choose a partner whose people had fought with yours years ago." Mr. Owens smiled. "That way, we can show that old wars and arguments mean nothing today." He looked around the class. "People from different heritages can become friends. Does everyone understand what I mean?" he asked.

A chorus of "Yes, Mr. Owens," and "Uh-huhs" filled the air. Sam tightened his mouth. He couldn't think of any reason for anyone to pick him.

So who would be his partner? That was easy to answer. No one would pick him because no one really knew him. Everyone would pick friends for partners—no matter what Mr. Owens said. That's just how it always was.

Just then, Jack walked by his desk. He stopped and looked at Sam's drawing.

"Not bad," Jack said. "What's your report on?" he asked.

"My grandfather," Sam muttered. Please, don't ask why, he begged silently.

"Oh, yeah?" Jack said. "How come? Was he in pro ball, like mine?" Jack puffed out his chest.

Sam wanted to slide down in his desk. "Uh—no," he mumbled. "He—uh—was in World War II."

"Oh, yeah?" Jack said. He looked interested. "A war hero, huh?" He leaned on Sam's desk. "How many medals did he win?"

"None," Sam croaked.

"None? None?" Jack asked unbelievingly. He began to grin.

"So why are you proud of him? Was he a famous pilot or something?"

"He—he was a prisoner," Sam choked out.

Jack began to laugh. "Proud of a prisoner? You're proud of a prisoner?"

Sam didn't know if he wanted to punch Jack or just hide under his desk. Kids nearby began to look over and stare.

"Sit down and get to work," Mr. Owens called out. "These are all due tomorrow, remember." Grinning, Jack strutted over to his desk.

Sam felt his forehead bead up in sweat. He shouldn't let someone like Jack make him mad.

"The secret to survival," he could still hear Zaydeh say, "is not letting them **get your goat**." Then Zaydeh would smile at Sam and muss his hair.

Sam blew some eraser dust off one of his pictures. He had drawn pictures of the prison camp, of the barracks, of the mean guards, and of the other prisoners. He had drawn a picture of the soldier finding Zaydeh in the snow too. It was going to be a good report.

No one had to remind Sam the projects were due the next day. He had his yarmulke laid out and ready at home. Mom had bought two jars of kosher pickles for him to take to school. He could tell the kids that kosher meant that food had been fixed in a special way for Jewish people.

Sam's report was almost ready. He read his first paragraph to himself. "My grandfather said that bravery and courage led to liberation—that and the great U.S. Army."

Zaydeh used to say those words every time he began to tell one of his stories. Zaydeh had helped Sam with his report after all. A smile lit up Sam's face.

But the only thing he didn't have ready was his partner for Heritage Day. Sam knew he'd be by himself tomorrow. Or worse—with Mr. Owens. Mr. Owens was going to wear a costume.

He could just imagine having the whole school see the teacher as his partner! Sam made a face.

Everyone in the school would know he couldn't get a partner. Sam looked around the room at all the faces of his classmates. He had to get a partner. He just had to.

But how?

5
Heritage Day

The next morning, Sam carefully
put on his yarmulke. He looked in the
hall mirror to make sure the yarmulke
was in just the right place on his head.

"Is it okay?" Sam asked Mom.

"It's fine. Just relax and enjoy your day," Mom said. She put the last jar of pickles in a plastic bag.

Relax? Hah! Sam wanted to say out loud. But he didn't. He'd tried so hard last night to think how to get a partner for Heritage Day. How could he do it? He'd asked himself over and over, as he lay in bed. He had tried to keep his eyes open, but he finally fell asleep.

Sam made a face. All he could hope for was that maybe someone would be sick. Then there would be an even number of kids. But that probably wouldn't happen. Besides, Mom would say it wasn't nice to wish someone would get sick. Sam sighed and zipped the bags into his backpack.

"Thanks, Mom," he said, tucking his special project into the side pocket of the backpack.

Sam's mom dropped him off at school. He entered the building and walked slowly through the hall, dreading the day. If only it weren't Heritage Day, he'd feel better.

Sam hadn't wanted to go to school today. But Zaydeh would have told him, "Look on the bright side, Sam, don't **kvetch**." He always said that when things looked grim.

Well, at least they wouldn't have to do math and reading. Today they'd be eating different foods. They'd get to hear all of the projects. And his project was pretty good, even if he did say so himself. Sam smiled a little.

Then he remembered what Jack had said. "Proud of a prisoner?" he'd asked. So what? Sam told himself. Yes, he was proud of a prisoner.

Mom had let him use Zaydeh's

picture in his report. It looked great.

"Be very careful with this," Mom had said as she handed Sam the picture.

"I will. I promise," Sam had answered.

Sam felt a little better just looking at the picture of Zaydeh. If only he didn't have to be partners with Mr. Owens—in front of everyone in the whole school. He sighed.

Sam opened the door to the classroom. He was early. Mr. Owens sat at his desk. He wore a fancy embroidered vest and a shirt with long sleeves. Sachi was the only other person in the room. She was sitting at her desk bent over her work.

Sachi was wearing a lime green **kimono**. Her hair was pinned up on her head. She looked really different, Sam thought. Sachi looked up at him.

"Oh, hi, Sam," Sachi said. She frowned at her report lying on her desk.

"What's wrong?" Sam asked. He put down his backpack and looked at her report. Soldiers marched across her cover, and a few clouds sailed in the sky above.

"I'm still having trouble drawing an airplane on my report cover. The report's done. I just thought an airplane flying above the marching soldiers would look extra nice," Sachi said. She rested her chin in her hands and sighed, staring at her cover.

He could help, Sam thought quickly. Why not? He could help Sachi draw an airplane. So what if it didn't look exactly like a World War II plane?

But—should he even ask her? What if she said that she didn't want his help?

Sam could almost feel his face

turning red with embarrassment already. A schnook, he told himself. I'll look like a schnook.

Sachi rolled her pencil down her desktop and made a face. "I'm not good at drawing." She looked back at Sam and sighed.

Sam took a breath. Here goes, he thought. "I—maybe I could help you," Sam said, hesitantly. He held his breath and waited for Sachi's answer.

"Could you?" Sachi exclaimed. Her eyes lit up and she smiled. "Could you really?"

A little flash of happiness warmed Sam. "Uh—uh, sure," he managed to say. "I'll try, anyway."

Sam pushed his desk closer and took out a sheet of blank paper from his notebook. "Here," he said. "Draw the body of the plane like this." With a few, quick strokes of his pencil, a plane began to appear.

Sachi grinned in surprise. "Thanks! That's perfect! You make it look so easy," she said. She began copying his strokes on her cover. Wings and a nose took shape. Sam shaded the drawing under the wings. Sachi followed his lead.

She leaned back in her desk and smiled at her cover. "Hey, not bad," she said. She grinned at Sam. "Thanks a lot! I wish I could help you with something to pay you back," Sachi said. She looked over at his report. "But it doesn't look like you need any help at all."

I do need help—with baseball, Sam thought. He was actually getting tired of drawing at recess. Besides, he knew what Zaydeh would have wanted him to do.

All right. Here's my chance, Sam told himself. He would ask. Sachi wouldn't laugh at him, would she?

And, after all, he was helping her out, wasn't he? He took a deep breath.

"Um, I—I *do* need help," Sam said slowly. He looked down at his desk.

"With what?" Sachi asked. "Your report looks really good."

"With—with baseball," Sam said quickly, before he could change his mind.

"Ohhh," Sachi said. She grinned at him. "Is that why you don't watch us play anymore?"

Sam's heart sank to his shoes. Sachi *was* going to laugh at him. He knew it. He had made an awful mistake.

Sam looked up and saw a couple of students enter the room. Sachi would tell everyone. And she would giggle about how Sam didn't know how to play baseball. He could already hear the others snickering and laughing.

"What a dummy!" some would say.

"Not know how to play baseball!" others would laugh.

"He needs baseball lessons?" still others would ask.

Sam's face turned beet red. Now he'd really messed up.

"Sure!" Sachi said. "I'll help you." She grinned at him. "Come early before school. We'll throw together."

Relief flooded Sam. It was all right! She wasn't going to make fun of him!

"Thanks!" Sam said, gratefully.

Kids had begun streaming into the classroom. They were dressed in colorful costumes and carrying bags and trays of food with their backpacks. They wore flowing robes, long dresses, short pants, and flat hats. The classroom began to look like a celebration. Except Sam didn't feel like celebrating. He would have

Mr. Owens for a partner.

"What a loser," the kids would whisper. He just knew it.

"Can I see your report?" Sachi asked Sam.

Sam handed her his report. He watched as Sachi began to turn the pages, looking at the drawings. Suddenly she stopped.

"Wait a minute!" she exclaimed. She had stopped at the picture of Zaydeh and the soldier who rescued him. Her face looked funny.

"How did you get my picture?" she asked. She held up the page to show Sam. "What are you doing with my picture? Why did you take it out of my report?"

Sam sat very still. "Huh? What?" he asked. "What do you mean? *Your* picture?" he repeated. "I didn't take any picture of yours. That's my picture!"

"This is my picture of my grandfather," Sachi said. She pointed to the soldier holding onto Zaydeh.

"What?" Sam asked. But then he stared. The soldier was Japanese American. His heart began to thud under his shirt. It couldn't be, could it?

"Where is it?" Sachi asked as she quickly flipped pages in her report. Then she held up a page for Sam to see. She gasped. "Look!" she said excitedly. She pointed to a matching picture. There, right before Sam's eyes, was another picture just like Sam's of Zaydeh and his soldier-rescuer.

"I can't believe it!" Sam exclaimed. He sat, stunned for a second. "Your grandfather rescued my grandfather?" he said. Then his heart filled with excitement. Sachi's grandfather was Zaydeh's liberator!

That was why Sachi had seemed familiar.

Suddenly, Sam understood. "I forgot!" he burst out. "We're living back in his first U.S. hometown!"

"Oh my gosh!" Sachi said. "Mr. Owens! Mr. Owens!" she called out, jumping up from her desk.

"Mr. Owens! Mr. Owens!" Sam called out at the same time. Wait until Mom hears this! Sam thought.

"Guess what?" Sachi exclaimed to Mr. Owens. "You won't believe this! Come here!"

Everyone was staring at Sachi and Sam. Mr. Owens walked over quickly. The other students crowded around to hear Sachi and Sam explain the story.

"And my grandfather's 522nd Field Artillery **Battalion** of Japanese Americans was one of the bravest in the whole war," Sachi finished.

"And they liberated the **concentration camps** in Germany," Sam said. "They saved lives—like my zaydeh's. The prisoners were freed because of the soldiers."

Mr. Owens explained to the class, "The Japanese Americans volunteered to fight for their country, even though they had been put in prison camps in America."

Sam remembered this part, just as Zaydeh had told him. "They were arrested only because they were Japanese. The government took away their homes and their land," Sam said.

"But why?" asked a voice from the back of the group.

Mr. Owens answered. "The government said it was to protect the United States. We were fighting

Japan as well as Germany. But it was a terrible thing to do to our own citizens. The Japanese Americans fought to prove they were just as American as everyone else."

"Their troops won many medals," Sam added. "My zaydeh told me!"

Sachi smiled proudly at everyone.

"This is very special," Mr. Owens said. "I've heard many stories of how bravely the Japanese Americans fought in the war. Everyone has." He smiled at the class.

Then the teacher's smile faded. "And I've also heard many stories of how brave the Jewish prisoners were in the German concentration camps."

Mr. Owens looked at Sam and nodded his head. Sam's heart lifted. Mr. Owens knew about Zaydeh's bravery! Take that, Jack! Sam wanted to say. But he wanted Mr. Owens to tell the class more.

"They were taken from their homes and lost their land," Mr. Owens went on. "They were like the Japanese. But they were imprisoned and then killed only because they were Jews. The Germans said it was for the protection of Germany. But it was horribly wrong. In the camps, the prisoners helped one another."

Sam chimed in, "That's right. My zaydeh told me how they kept one another's spirits up. They took care of one another. It would have been easy to give up, but they didn't."

Mr. Owens smiled at Sam. "They were true heroes too. Everyone needs to remember the prisoners' courage."

Sam lifted his chin and smiled a little. For a moment, he imagined Zaydeh was standing right beside him.

"All right, class," Mr. Owens said,

"this would be a good time for everyone to choose partners. Be sure you give me the reason you chose your partner."

Sam's heart sank. Mr. Owens grabbed a red marker and began writing on the board as he called out kids' names. If only he'd been able to think of a plan. Now he was doomed.

"Murphy? LaShawn? Danielle? Ricardo?" he asked each student in turn, listening to their answers and writing names and reasons on the board.

"Sachi?" Mr. Owens finished. Sam had been counting. Only he, Sachi, and Jack had no partners yet. Here it came, he thought. He squeezed his eyes shut. Was anybody looking at him?

"Sam will be my partner," Sachi said.

Sam's eyes popped open. His jaw dropped. He stared at Sachi. He was going to be Sachi's partner?

"I choose Sam," Sachi said, lifting her chin, "because our grandfathers were brave together."

A rush of pride filled Sam. He would be partners with Sachi—just as their grandfathers had been partners.

"That's a great idea," Mr. Owens said, as he wrote *Sam and Sachi— Bravery* on the board. "Let's see," he said, turning around to look at the class. "That leaves Jack, who will be my partner." He smiled at Jack.

Sam hid a grin as he watched Jack turn bright red. Jack made a face when Mr. Owens turned his back.

"Let's begin sharing our heritage food, class," Mr. Owens said.

Talking and the sound of moving desks and tables filled the air while students set out their dishes.

Delicious smells drifted across the classroom. Sam could smell garlic, spices, and sweet scents. Sachi set out her musubi, or rice balls. Next to her, Sam struggled to open his jars of kosher pickles.

"Unnnh!" he gasped, straining as he tried to twist the slippery lid open.

POP! The jar lid snapped off. Pickle juice flew into the air.

"Oh, no!" Sachi wailed, looking down at her kimono.

Sam looked over at her kimono too. Now he'd really done it! He had just put a kibosh on his wonderful day!

"I—I'm sorry!" he stammered.

Dribbles of pickle juice trickled down Sachi's kimono. At least the juice was almost the same color, Sam sighed to himself. Then Sam saw Sachi smiling.

"Don't worry," she said. "You can't even see it."

Sam let his breath out. He smiled at Sachi.

"You know what?" he asked Sachi. "Now you have a kosher kimono!"

Sachi and Sam looked at each other, and they began to laugh.

Later, all the partners prepared to give their presentations. Sachi and Sam were first.

"A kosher kimono," Sachi giggled to Sam when they marched to the front of the classroom.

"That's the best kind of all," Sam said with a grin. And he knew Zaydeh and Sachi's grandfather—their secret heroes—would think so too.

Afterword

Some Real Secret Heroes

Sachi and Sam's story is based on a real event. The 522nd Field Artillery Battalion unit liberated the Dachau concentration camp in Bavaria in May 1945.

The Germans had taken the Jewish prisoners from the camp and into the Bavarian Alps on a death march. The Germans were hoping to escape from the nearby Americans, who were chasing them.

Two-thirds of the prisoners had already died by the time the 522nd found them. The Japanese American soldiers of the 522nd freed the Jewish prisoners from a terrible prison camp.

It is amazing to realize that the Japanese American soldiers' own families had to live in prison camps back in the United States. Still, many Japanese Americans fought for the United States during World War II. They fought bravely to prove their loyalty to their country. These soldiers were real heroes.

Today, people can become U.S. citizens no matter where they are born. That was not true for the Japanese Americans after World War II until 1952.

The Japanese immigrants who came to the United States before 1952 couldn't even become citizens because they weren't born in the United States—a country they loved. For years, many people in the

United States had looked down on Japanese Americans because of their ancestry.

Even so, they loved their new country. Their children—Japanese Americans born in the United States—were citizens by birth. Sadly, even they were treated badly. But the Japanese Americans still worked hard, got good educations, and contributed to the United States.

Then Japan bombed Pearl Harbor, Hawaii, on December 7, 1941. The United States declared war on Japan. All Japanese American citizens and noncitizens were suddenly considered enemies. It didn't matter that they had been born in the United States and were Americans.

In 1942, President Roosevelt ordered a **relocation** of Japanese Americans from their homes in the western United States to **internment camps**. This order forced 120,000 Japanese Americans to leave their homes, businesses, and lives behind. They lost everything they had worked for.

The Japanese Americans spent the war years behind barbed wire fences, living in bleak **barracks**. It was a terrible time.

But the Japanese Americans wanted to prove their loyalty to the United States, even though their own country put them behind bars. More than 30,000 Japanese Americans volunteered to serve in the war against Japan, Italy, and Germany. Many heroes can be found in the stories of the Japanese Americans in the battalions and in the Military Intelligence Service.

The Japanese American 442nd Regiment was the most-decorated regiment in U.S. history for its size and length of service. The 522nd Field Artillery was a proud part of this regiment. Sachi and Sam can be proud of their secret heroes.

Glossary

barracks housing
characterized by
its extreme
plainness

battalion military group with
a headquarters and
three or more
smaller groups

betray to be disloyal to a
person or country

bubbie Yiddish word for
"grandmother"

concentration camp	prison camp used for holding civilians in times of war
cubby	small storage compartment
get your goat	to get angry or annoyed
internment camp	place for the confinement of people considered a security threat, especially during a war

kibosh	something that puts a stop on something else
kimono	loose, floor-length, traditional Japanese garment that has wide sleeves, wraps in front, and is fastened with a sash
kosher	relating to food that has been prepared so that it is fit and suitable under Jewish law
kvetch	to grumble and complain about things all the time

liberation	process of being set free
Louvre	famous museum in Paris, France, that contains the national art collection
matzo ball	small dumpling made from matzo meal
meshuga	crazy or foolish
relocation	act of moving people to a new place on a long-term basis

reunion	gathering of old friends, relatives, or people who worked together
schlepp	to drag or haul
schmo	annoying person
schnook	stupid or unimportant person
scrawny	unhealthily thin and bony
scuff	to beat badly

shtick	person's special trait, talent, or interest
yarmulke	small round cap worn by Jewish men and boys
zaydeh	Yiddish word for "grandfather"

About the Authors

Carla Mishek was born and raised in Los Angeles, California. She received her degree from Immaculate Heart of Mary College after which she taught in elementary schools connected with the Los Angeles Unified School District.

Ms. Mishek and her late husband, Ron, moved to Eugene, Oregon, where they lived for almost seven years. She has since returned to her home state where she does volunteer work with local children in Irvine, California.

Her love of writing has dominated her professional life and retirement. A devotion to animals has never waned and is a part of her concerns and hopes.

One of Ms. Mishek's stories appeared in *Spider's* September 2002 magazine. Its title is "Rosalinda's Special Gift."

• • •

Margo Sorenson was born in Washington, D.C. She spent the first seven years of her life in Europe, living where there were few children her age. She found books to be her best friends and read constantly. Ms. Sorenson wrote her own stories too.

Ms. Sorenson finished her school years in California, graduating from the University of California at Los Angeles. She taught high school and middle school and raised a family of two daughters. Ms. Sorenson is now a full-time writer, writing primarily for young people.

After having lived in Hawaii, Minnesota, and California, Ms. Sorenson now lives in California with her husband. When she isn't writing, she enjoys reading, sports, and traveling.